Kenny usually looked sure of himself. But his dark eyes looked worried now as he stared at the pitcher. His muscles twitched as he cocked the bat high.

"Relax, Kenny," Jacob shouted. "Just *meet* the ball."

It was the advice Kenny usually gave to Jacob.

Coach Wilkens put his hands to his mouth and yelled, "Take it easy, Kenny. Don't press."

And then Jacob found himself falling into his old habit—pretending to broadcast the game.

"Yes, fans, the great Kenny Sandoval, all-star and future major leaguer, is up to bat. He's had some bad luck today, but he's due to turn things around any minute."

Kenny took a hard swing...and missed.

Look for these books about the
Angel Park All-Stars

WINNING STREAK

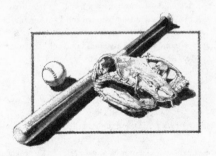

By Dean Hughes

Illustrated by Dennis Lyall

BULLSEYE BOOKS • RANDOM HOUSE
NEW YORK

A BULLSEYE BOOK PUBLISHED BY RANDOM HOUSE, INC.
Copyright © 1990 by Dean Hughes
Cover art copyright © 1990 by Rick Ormond
Interior illustrations copyright © 1990 by Dennis Lyall
ANGEL PARK ALL-STARS characters copyright © 1989 by Alfred A. Knopf, Inc.

Library of Congress Cataloging-in-Publication Data:
Hughes, Dean, 1943–
Winning streak / by Dean Hughes ; illustrated by Dennis Lyall.
p. cm. — (Angel Park all-stars ; 3)
Summary: Kenny, the rookie star of Angel Park's Little League baseball team,
finds himself in a major slump because he's trying too hard.
[1. Baseball—Fiction.] I. Lyall, Dennis, ill. II. Title. III. Series: Hughes, Dean,
1943– Angel Park all-stars ; 3.
PZ7.H87312Wi 1990
[Fic]—dc20 89-24033
ISBN 0-679-90428-X (lib. bdg.) — ISBN 0-679-80428-5 (pbk.)
RL: 2.6
First Bullseye Books edition: 1990
Manufactured in the United States of America   10 9 8 7 6 5 4

for Nicelle Hughes

★ 1 ★

Bad Hop

===

Jacob felt the baseball connect—*solid*. And then he watched it shoot toward the gap in left-center. The outfielders raced after it, but the ball bounced and rolled to the fence.

Jacob made the turn at first and kept on running. He wanted to slide into second but didn't have to. Instead, he jogged the last few steps and jumped on the bag with both feet.

Then he turned and watched Billy Bacon cross the plate.

Rodney Bunson, who had scored from

second, was waiting. He slapped hands with Billy, and the two trotted to the dugout.

Jacob had himself a double *and* two runs-batted-in.

"Yeah!" he shouted. And then he shot both fists into the air.

His best friends, Harlan Sloan and Kenny Sandoval—the other rookies on the team—waved and shouted. In fact, all the Dodgers were yelling.

"Don't mess with our third-graders," Sterling Malone, the Dodgers' big center fielder, yelled. "They're *power*-hitters."

But it wasn't just the rookies. Everyone was hitting. The team was as hot as the weather this Saturday morning. It was only the third inning and the score was already 8 to 2, Dodgers over the Padres. The Angel Park team was well on its way to another win.

And that would make six in a row with *no* losses!

Best of all, for the first time Jacob Scott had been put in the starting lineup. And he had really delivered.

Henry White, the third baseman and leadoff man, was coming up to bat. He already had two singles in the game. Jacob was sure Henry would drive him in.

But this time Henry bounced a grounder to the shortstop.

Jacob had to hold at second.

Jeff Reinhold did no better. He swung late and trickled a ball down the first-base line.

Jacob ran to third on the fielder's choice, but Jeff was out.

And now Kenny Sandoval was up.

Kenny was about the only Dodger who hadn't had a hit. And Jacob knew he wanted one.

He was also one of the best players on the team, even though he was only nine, like Jacob. But the week before, against the Reds, he had suddenly stopped hitting—after being hot the first four games of the season.

And today, nothing had gone right.

The first time up he had hit the ball hard, almost knocking down the Padres' pitcher. But the kid had raised his glove and the ball had stuck.

The second time up, Kenny had hit two long shots—both foul—and then struck out on a pitch that wasn't even in the strike zone.

Kenny usually looked sure of himself. But his dark eyes looked worried now as he stared at the pitcher. His muscles twitched as he cocked the bat high.

"Relax, Kenny," Jacob shouted. "Just *meet* the ball."

It was the advice Kenny usually gave to Jacob.

Coach Wilkens put his hands to his mouth and yelled, "Take it easy, Kenny. Don't press."

And then Jacob found himself falling into his old habit—pretending to broadcast the game.

"Yes, fans, the great Kenny Sandoval, all-star and future major leaguer, is up to bat. He's had some bad luck today, but he's due to turn things around any minute."

Kenny took a hard swing . . . and missed.

Jacob's voice always sounded too big coming from such a small guy—especially a freckle-faced kid with a gap-toothed grin. But he raised that big voice now. "That's right, Frank. He's acting awful nervous. He's a-squeezin' that ol' bat like he's trying to choke it to death."

Maybe he could get Kenny to laugh. And relax a little.

But Kenny was paying no attention.

Swiiiinngggg.

Another miss. He had really lunged at the ball.

"No, Kenny," his mother yelled from the

crowd. "Don't try to kill the ball. Let up a little."

Kenny nodded, as if to answer his mom, but then he stepped back into the box and took the same kind of swing again.

"Steeee-rike three!"

Kenny slammed his bat on the ground and spun around. Jacob jogged toward him.

"Kenny, you're trying too hard to—"

"I *know* what I'm doing," Kenny said. "It's stupid. I don't know why I can't stop my-self."

The two jogged back to the dugout to-gether. Mr. Sandoval had come down to the fence. "Hey, son," he said, "remember you're playing a game. Have some fun. You'll play better that way."

Kenny told his dad he would, and then he ran out to his position at shortstop and fielded the ground balls that Jenny threw him. He scooped them up and made good throws to first. Jacob thought that maybe Kenny had taken his dad's advice.

The first batter looked bad on a couple of swings, but then he crunched a hard grounder right at Kenny.

Kenny took a step toward the ball and got in front of it—just the way the coach always said to. He looked smooth and natural as he bent and watched the ball right into his—

And then the ball took a crazy hop right over his glove.

And hit him in the face!

Kenny went down, scrambled back to his feet quickly, and looked for the ball.

But Henry White had already hustled after it. Henry eyed the runner, who held at first.

"Time out!" Coach Wilkens yelled, and he ran onto the field.

Kenny had slumped to his knees.

Jacob was running toward him from right field, and so were the players in the infield. Harlan Sloan charged out from the dugout.

"Are you okay?" the coach was saying as

Jacob reached the little group that had collected around Kenny.

"Yeah. I'm okay. I can keep playing. It just made me dizzy for a second."

"Where did it hit you?"

"In the forehead."

Jacob could see the red mark just above Kenny's right eye.

Mr. Sandoval was walking onto the field now. "Is he okay?" he asked.

Coach Wilkens stood up. "I think so. But it might be a good idea to take him home and get him out of this heat. A knock like that could cause a concussion."

"Yeah. I think that's a good idea."

"I want to play," Kenny said. He stood up. "I'm fine."

But his dad took him by the arm and led him off the field. The crowd gave him a nice hand.

Mrs. Sandoval met Kenny as he crossed the foul line. "You poor guy," she said.

Harlan was standing next to Jacob. The

two of them watched as Kenny's parents led him back to Mrs. Sandoval's car. "Man, I can't believe the lousy luck Kenny's having lately," Harlan said.

"He's in a bad slump," Jacob said.

"No, I think he just—"

"Believe me, it's a slump. And we've got to do something about it."

"Do something? What can *we* do?"

"We're his best friends, aren't we?"

"Sure. But I don't see what we can—"

"We've got to change his luck. That's what we've got to do."

Harlan was staring at Jacob, sort of half smiling with those big teeth of his, and his big ears were sticking out from under his baseball cap. "What?" he said.

"Geez, Harlan," Jacob said, "don't you know anything about baseball? There are ways to break out of a slump. We can't just sit by and let our friend's whole season go down the drain."

★ 2 ★

No Luck

The Dodgers won the game, 11 to 5, and
their streak was still alive.

But the team had looked bad in the late
innings. The defense had made some
errors and the pitchers had walked too
many.

Coach Wilkens told the players they had
let up. They would have to do a lot better
against the Giants.

After the game Harlan and Jacob walked
over to Kenny's house.

"You don't know how serious this thing
with Kenny could be," Jacob told Harlan.

Jacob was still wearing his baseball glove—but then, he almost never took it off. Now he pounded his fist into the pocket. "A slump can keep getting worse and worse."

"He'll do okay next time."

"Maybe. But we can't depend on that. I know some of the stuff major leaguers do to break out of slumps."

They were walking past Mr. Aragon's store, Angel Park Drug.

"Let's see whether they have any rabbit's feet," Jacob said.

"Jacob, that's stupid," Harlan said. "Stuff like that doesn't do any good."

But Jacob was serious. He walked in and asked Mr. Aragon whether he carried any lucky charms.

Mr. Aragon laughed. "Well, no," he said. "I don't go in much for that sort of thing. Maybe you ought to try practicing more."

"It's not for me," Jacob said. "It's for a friend of mine. He's in a slump."

Jacob leaned on the glass case with his elbows. He felt sort of out of place in his baseball uniform.

"Well, I don't know what to tell you," Mr. Aragon said, and he chuckled. "Maybe you can switch uniforms with him. That number six is pretty lucky, I think."

"Maybe," Jacob said. It was a thought. "But he's a lot taller than I am."

"Come on, Jacob," Harlan said. "Let's go."

Jacob sighed. He could see that he was getting nowhere.

But as they walked out the door Mr. Aragon called out, "Have him change his shirt. The big leaguers do that."

Jacob nodded. "See. He does know something about baseball," he said to Harlan.

"Changing shirts may not help them *play* better, but they *smell* better," Mr. Aragon yelled, and then he laughed.

Harlan laughed too. Jacob didn't.

Kenny's mom said he had to stay inside and rest. Kenny said he was fine. All he wanted to do was take a little batting practice. But he did have quite a knot over his eye.

"Right now, practice isn't what you need," Jacob said. "You need to *change* everything."

"What?" Kenny was sitting on his bed, staring down at Jacob, who was on the floor, leaning against the bedroom wall.

Harlan was sitting backward on a chair, his long legs spread around the chairback. He started to laugh again. "He thinks you're in a slump," he said.

"Well, he *is*. Anyone can see that."

"What are you talking about?" Kenny said. "I just messed up a couple of times."

"You haven't had a hit in two games."

"I know. But I hit the ball hard a couple of times. I just had some bad luck."

"Exactly!" Jacob said. "Bad luck. And that's what we have to change. Don't worry, though. I know how to do this. I've heard

all about the stuff the major leaguers do."

"You mean like rubbing the catcher's head and stuff like that?"

Now it was Harlan who was saying, "What?"

But Jacob paid no attention. "Sure. That's good. The pros all do that. But mainly you have to change your whole routine."

"What routine? I don't have a routine."

"Sure you do. Everyone does. I'll come over before the game on Wednesday and help you mix all that stuff up."

"Mix what stuff up?"

"You gotta change your undershirt and your socks, and—"

"Hey, I always change my underwear. Don't you?"

"That's not what I'm talking about, stupid. You can't just wash that stuff and put it back on. Not when you're in a slump. You have to stop wearing it. You have to try some new things."

Kenny was shaking his head. "No way, Jacob. I don't need to do that. I'll do okay next time."

"I'm not taking no for an answer. You helped me when I couldn't get a hit. Now I'm sticking with you. That's what buddies are for."

Jacob grinned. Harlan laughed. Kenny was shaking his head again.

On Wednesday Jacob walked home from school with Kenny. He watched everything Kenny was about to do, and then made him change it somehow.

When Kenny started to put his uniform top on, Jacob stopped him and made him put the pants on first.

When he got some socks out of a drawer, Jacob made him find a pair he hadn't worn all season.

When he got his sweatbands out, Jacob made him leave them home.

And when he started to make himself a peanut butter sandwich, Jacob made him switch to tuna fish.

Kenny put up with all of it. And then he agreed to walk the long way to the Little League park. He even agreed to put a penny in his shoe. But when Jacob told him he had to choose a new bat, Kenny finally put his foot down.

"No way, Jacob. I've had a lot of hits with that bat. If I struck out last time, it's not the bat's fault."

"Kenny, that's the first thing the pros change when they get into a slump. It's probably the most important thing you can do."

"Nope. I'm not doing it."

"Well, then, at least wear a rally hat."

"A what?"

"When you're in the dugout, put your hat on upside down like this." Jacob turned his inside out and crushed it onto his head, so it looked like it was ready to catch rain. "Or turn it around. Or something. Or hold it and shake it."

"Jacob, that's nutty. I'd look like a goof walking around like that."

"The greatest players in the world do it, Kenny. Don't you know about rally hats?"

"I know about swinging a bat right. That's what I'm going to do."

But once the game had started and it was Kenny's turn at bat, he walked out to the plate with his hat on the normal way.

"This is going to be a disaster," Jacob told Harlan.

And then he yelled out to Kenny. "Don't take your regular number of practice swings. Take a few more. Or not so many."

But Kenny wasn't listening.

He stepped up to the plate and went into his usual stance, standing back in the box, his bat held high and still, the heel of his left foot lifted just a little. He looked powerful, but Jacob knew it would never work.

Crack.

Kenny lashed a line drive—like a rope—to left field.

"ALL RIGHT!!!" Jacob screamed. He jumped up and watched as Kenny raced toward first base.

"I told you. I told you," Jacob shouted to Harlan. "All that stuff we did—it changed his luck."

Kenny rounded first and took a few quick bluff steps toward second, but then he eased off. Just as he was about to stop and trot back into first his legs somehow tangled, and suddenly he was on his face in the dirt.

The shortstop had just taken the relay throw from the girl in left field. "First base. First base," all the other infielders yelled.

The shortstop spun and threw to first, and then the first baseman put the tag on Kenny before he could scramble back to the base.

"*OUT!!!!!!!*" the umpire bellowed.

"*Oh, NOOOOOO,*" Jacob moaned, and he crashed back down on the bench. "I don't believe it."

"Tough break," Harlan mumbled.

"I knew he should have worn a rally hat," Jacob said. "Why won't the guy listen to me?"

BOX SCORE, GAME 6

Santa Rita Padres 5

	ab	r	h	rbi
Roberts 2b	4	1	3	2
Brown lf	2	1	0	0
Jorgensen ss	3	0	1	1
Durkin 1b	3	0	1	1
Cegielski c	3	1	0	0
Blough 3b	2	0	1	0
Valenciano p	1	1	0	0
Brenchley rf	2	0	1	0
Shimer cf	3	0	0	0
Nakatani lf	2	0	1	1
Orosco rf	2	1	1	0
Kim cf	2	0	0	0
ttl	**29**	**5**	**9**	**5**

Angel Park Dodgers 11

	ab	r	h	rbi
White 3b	4	2	2	0
Reinhold 2b	2	1	1	1
Sandoval ss	4	0	0	0
Malone cf	3	2	2	4
Boschi lf	4	1	1	0
Roper 1b	2	0	1	1
Bunson p	3	1	1	0
Bacon c	2	2	2	2
Scott rf	1	1	1	2
Waters rf	1	0	0	0
Sloan 1b	1	1	1	0
Sandia ss	1	0	0	0
	28	**11**	**12**	**10**

Padres   0 2 0   2 1 0—5
Dodgers 3 3 2   3 0 x—11

From Bad to Wurst

Kenny's bad luck was only the beginning. Suddenly nothing seemed to go right for the Dodgers. Bunson still wasn't really his old self—he was still having trouble with the ankle he'd sprained a few games back. And the Giants were tough hitters.

In the second inning Bunson walked two batters and then gave up a double that scored them both.

In the third inning he gave up a single to the left fielder. Then their star third baseman—a kid named David Weight—hit a high drive over the fence.

Four to nothing.

And the Dodgers got *zip* again in the bottom of the inning.

Bunson was hanging on, but struggling. The Giants were all over him, and he was trying hard to control his temper.

In the top of the fourth he got the Giants out without giving up any more runs—in spite of a walk and an error—but in the fifth, he walked the first two batters.

Coach Wilkens came out and put Kenny in to pitch.

Bunson wasn't exactly happy about the idea, but he didn't throw a fit the way he had earlier in the year. "Get 'em out," he said to Kenny as he walked away.

Jacob was now in the game in right field and Harlan had taken over first base. Neither had been up to bat yet.

Jacob watched Kenny. He could see how tight he was. As Kenny warmed up he tried to throw too hard. He didn't look natural.

After the first inning mess-up, things hadn't gotten any better for Kenny. His good swing seemed to be gone, and Halliday had struck him out in the third inning again.

And then Kenny went out to play shortstop and let a ground ball go right through his legs.

Now he had to pitch, and he was forcing the ball, trying to put too much on it.

"What a slump," Jacob mumbled to himself. "I gotta think of a way to help the poor guy."

He spoke in his announcer's voice. "Frank, this rookie is a fine young pitcher, but he looks a little nervous to me.

"Yes, I know what you mean, Hank. He just tried to spit, but the only thing that came out was powdered sugar."

"That's it!" Jacob told himself. "I've got to get serious about making him laugh."

Suddenly, Jacob ran toward the pitcher's mound. "Time out," he yelled.

"Time *is* out," the umpire said.

"Oh, yeah."

Jacob ran over to Kenny, who was getting ready to take his final warm-up pitch.

"Kenny," he said, "have you smelled Cranny today? He smells like . . . a dirty pair of socks."

Kenny didn't laugh. "What?"

"That guy's a real hot dog. He's the wurst." It was a joke Jacob had read in one of those stale joke books.

"Jacob, get back to your position. What are you doing?"

"You gotta lighten up, Kenny. You're throwing too hard."

"Yeah, and I should turn my hat upside down while I pitch."

"Couldn't hurt." Jacob grinned.

Kenny turned around.

Jacob felt stupid, but he trotted back to right field and waited for the next disaster.

Kenny let fly with his first pitch, which

shot over Billy's head all the way to the screen.

The two runners moved up.

Kenny kicked at the pitching rubber, and then he fired a pitch that was inside and low. Billy was lucky to stop it.

Jacob yelled to Kenny, "Take it easy. Just throw strikes." But he knew that was stupid. Kenny was *trying* to throw strikes.

The Giants were riding Kenny worse than anyone had all year. They hadn't forgotten that he had been the guy who had gotten the big hits to beat them last time—and he had pitched too.

Cranny was turning up the heat. "Hey, little boy," he kept yelling. "What are you doing wearing your big brother's uniform? You're too little to play this game."

The truth was, Kenny was almost a head taller than Cranny, but Cranny seemed to ignore that.

Kenny took a long breath. Jacob knew he

was trying to settle himself down. Kenny brought his hands to his chest, checked the runners, and then reared back and fired. The ball barely missed the strike zone.

"Come on, ump," Jacob heard Jenny Roper yell from the dugout. "That ball was in there."

Jacob thought so too.

But there was no question about the next one. Kenny tried to aim the ball and threw a pitch that skidded in the dirt. Billy had to smother it to keep it from getting past him.

And now the bases were loaded.

Kenny walked off the mound and looked out toward center field. All the Dodgers were yelling at him to settle down.

"What's the matter, little third-grader?" Cranny was yelling. "Are you scared?"

The bleachers were full of Giants' fans. They were yelling for another home run. Weight was up again, and he could hit the ball as far as anyone.

Jacob knew what Kenny was feeling. All

the pressure was on his shoulders. He just *had* to throw strikes.

Kenny went back to the mound and took another breath. He pitched from the stretch position. Jacob could see he was softening his motion, just trying to get the ball over. But the ball looped high and had nothing on it.

The next pitch was low but outside.

And the one after that was high again.

The Giants in the dugout were laughing and shouting, and the base runners were working Kenny over. "Where's the plate, little kid? You can't even see it."

"Who told you you could pitch, little kid?"

Kenny came to his set position and checked the runners. Jacob could see how tight he looked. He was as stiff as a statue.

One more deep breath, and then Kenny rocked way back and fired.

But the motion was all wrong. The pitch almost hit the batter.

Weight ran to first base, laughing and

shouting, "Just keep walking us, Sandoval. That's okay with us."

The runner from third trotted across home plate. "Thanks for the nice walk around the bases," he yelled.

Kenny's problem hadn't changed. The bases were still loaded, and he still had to throw strikes.

But Coach Wilkens had seen enough. He put his hand on Kenny's shoulder and talked to him for quite a while. Jacob hoped the coach would think of the right thing to say.

Then he looked over at Harlan. Harlan shrugged and shook his head. Even he was starting to worry now.

Coach Wilkens took the ball from Kenny and waved for Eddie Boschi to come in from left field.

The coach didn't even send Kenny back to the field. Instead, he had Jenny come back into the game at first and sent Harlan to left.

Kenny walked to the dugout. The Giants laughed and made fun of him. When he sat down next to Bunson on the bench, he stared straight ahead. Jacob had never seen him look so down.

★ 4 ★

Too Little, Too Late

Boschi got the Giants out. The only trouble was, he gave up two more runs doing it.

The score was 7 to 0 going into the top of the sixth. Jacob couldn't see any hope in sight. Kenny was still in a slump—and now it seemed to be spreading to the whole team.

Luck was like that. Jacob had heard the big-league Dodgers' announcers talk about the way a slump could spread like measles.

"Hey, you guys, let's try some rally hats," Jacob told the players in the dugout. "Put your hats on like this." He turned his hat upside down and backward.

"Lay off, Jacob," Sterling said. "This isn't funny."

"I know. I'm serious. Big-leaguers do stuff like that all the time."

"Let's just get some hits," Jeff said. He was outside the dugout, looking for his bat. "They're taking Halliday out. Maybe we can hit their other pitchers."

That was good news. But seven runs to tie?

Jeff did what he had to do. He hit the ball on the nose and into center. When he got to first, he yelled, "All right, let's get it going. We can hit this guy."

But it was all a little hard to believe.

The Giants didn't believe it. They laughed when Eddie came up to bat. "Hey, *stork*," the first baseman yelled, "the only thing worse than your pitching is your hitting."

"Hey, first baseman," Bill Bacon yelled, "the only thing worse than your sweaty socks is your *breath*."

"Oh, yeah? Well, I can smell you all the way—"

CLICK.

Eddie laced a high fastball past the third baseman.

The left fielder hustled in and held Eddie to a single, and Jeff stopped at second.

"Hey, we can *do* this," Henry White yelled. "Come on, Jenny. It's *rally* time."

Jenny was striding toward home plate. She meant business. She pushed her helmet down tight, swung a couple of times, and settled in, her bat held almost straight back.

She took a pitch, and then she hit a ground ball deep to short. The guy hustled into the hole, gloved the ball, and tried to flip it to third for the force. But the ball bounced in front of the bag.

"*Safe!*" the umpire barked.

Bases loaded. More important, there were still no outs.

"*Hey!* We can *do* this!" Henry was yelling again. And everyone was joining in.

Jacob could feel the excitement. "Well, fans," he announced, "as the saying goes, the game ain't over 'til it's *over*. And those Giants better remember that."

The Dodgers all cheered. The Giants' smart-mouthed first baseman—a tall kid with a filthy uniform—gave them a phony grin to show he wasn't worried. But he was start-ing to think, Jacob figured.

The bottom of the order was coming up for the Dodgers. Billy was a pretty good hitter, but he wasn't very fast. And Jacob was on deck. He was already getting ner-vous.

Maybe the pitcher was too.

Billy fouled off the first pitch, and then took a couple. And then a ball got away from the pitcher and knicked Billy on the arm. "Take your base!" the umpire hollered.

One run in. Bases still loaded.

"We're *going* to do this," Henry yelled.

The Giants' first baseman kicked the bag. He wasn't smiling now.

Jacob was feeling the pressure though. He didn't want to let the team down.

The first pitch was fat and belt high. He swung but didn't get it all, rolling a grounder to the second baseman.

He ran hard but had a sinking feeling inside. Now there would be one out and—

The second baseman booted the ball!

It rolled away and he ran after it. By that time Eddie had scored and everyone was safe.

Seven to two.

They still had a mountain to climb, but it really did seem possible now. The Dodgers were all going nuts. Henry was coming up, and he *knew* he could do it.

But the Giants' coach was waving in a new pitcher from left field. He was a big guy named Sanchez. Jacob had seen him pitch.

He could be wild, but he could also throw hard.

While he was warming up, the Dodgers were psyching themselves. A few players even tried rally hats. But that worried Jacob. Luck was on their side—no use changing things now.

Jacob looked over at Kenny in the dugout and thought he knew what he was thinking. He was out of the game, and all he wanted was another chance.

But Kenny only clapped his hands and yelled to Henry, "Keep it going. Keep it going."

And Henry did. He didn't try to crush the ball. Instead, he timed a pitch just right and punched a single into center.

Jenny scored, and clapped her hands as she ran back to the dugout. *"Everybody* hits!" she yelled.

Jacob had moved up to second.

"Sterling Malone now represents the tying

run," he announced. "If he could sock one out of here, he could even things up."

The Giant shortstop told him to shut up, but Jacob only laughed and kept broadcasting.

Henry was yelling from first, "Don't try to knock the fence down, Sterling. Let's just keep the rally going."

The first baseman wasn't saying a word now. Jacob thought he looked a little sick.

Sterling took a pitch for a strike. He shook his head, disgusted with himself, and then got ready again. He took a perfect swing, but he hit the ball high in the air. The right fielder went back a few steps and made the catch.

Billy tagged up and came home to score and Jacob cruised into third, but now there was an out.

Jacob saw that some of the Giants' confidence had returned. "Come on, just two more," they were all yelling.

Danny Sandia was halfway to the batter's box before the coach called him back. "Kenny, bat for Danny," he called out. "And don't try to muscle the ball."

Kenny was going to get another chance after all.

Jacob was sure he could do it. But he wondered about his luck. "Kenny, try a different bat," he yelled.

Kenny wasn't listening.

Jacob saw the look in his eye. Kenny didn't look worried now. He had made up his mind what he had to do.

Kenny stepped into the box and pumped his bat until the pitcher came set. Then he coiled his arms and waited for the pitch.

The pitcher threw a ball outside and low.

Kenny stayed in the box, ready.

And on the next pitch he connected, driving the ball high and deep to straight-away center. Jacob turned and watched.

The center fielder went back . . . back . . . back . . .

To the fence.

The ball was arcing beyond the fence, it seemed, when the center fielder leaped, reached high.

And caught the ball!

The Dodgers had all been standing, breathless, ready to cheer.

For a few seconds they kept staring. They couldn't believe he had caught it.

"Tag up and score," Coach Wilkens yelled.

Jacob suddenly remembered where he was. He tagged the base and then ran home. But he could see how disappointed the other Dodgers were.

The Giants were yelling, "Two away. Two away."

"We can still do this," Henry yelled. The score was 7 to 5, and the coach was calling for Bunson to come back into the game.

"We're still going to get 'em," he yelled to his team. They all cheered. But it was scary now. Two outs and only one on.

Bunson had to come through.

He stepped up to the plate and dug in. He looked like he was ready to knock one downtown. And he swung hard—maybe too hard. He squibbed a weak ground ball back to the pitcher.

Sanchez grabbed it and ran most of the way to first before he flipped the ball to the first baseman.

Suddenly it was over. The first baseman shook the ball at Bunson and laughed. The other Giant players were jumping all over each other, going crazy.

It was something Jacob hadn't had to watch before. And it wasn't fun.

BOX SCORE, GAME 7

Blue Springs Giants   7

	ab	r	h	rbi
Glenn 1b	3	0	1	0
Sanchez lf	3	2	1	0
Villareal ss	3	1	1	0
Weight 3b	2	3	1	2
Cooper 2b	1	1	0	0
Halliday p	2	0	0	0
Zonn rf	2	0	1	2
Crandall c	2	0	2	1
Dodero cf	3	0	0	0
Hausberg 1b	1	0	0	0
Nugent 2b	1	0	0	1
Spinner rf	0	0	0	1
ttl	23	7	7	7

Angel Park Dodgers   5

	ab	r	h	rbi
White 3b	3	0	2	1
Malone cf	2	0	0	1
Sandoval ss	2	0	1	1
Bunson p	3	0	0	0
Reinhold 2b	3	1	1	0
Boschi lf	2	1	1	0
Roper 1b	3	1	1	0
Bacon c	2	1	0	1
Waters rf	1	0	0	0
Scott rf	1	1	1	0
Sandia ss	2	0	0	0
Sloan 1b	1	0	0	0
	25	5	7	4

Giants	0 2 2	0 3	0—7
Dodgers	0 0 0	0 0	5—5

★5★

What Are We Made Of?

"Come on, now. This isn't the end of the world."

Coach Wilkens was standing up and all the players were sitting on the grass. "It would have been nice not to lose all year, but it wasn't very likely to happen."

"We're in a slump," Jacob said.

"No, we're not," the coach said. He laughed. "Hey, it's just one game."

But no one laughed with him.

"That Halliday kid is tough to hit," the coach said. "But we got him once and we can get him again. It's the Reds we're tied with now. We each have one loss. We've got to get ready and beat them next time. And we gotta get the A's on Saturday."

"We can beat the A's any day," Danny Sandia said.

"You start talking that way and you might get taught a lesson," Coach Wilkens said. "The A's have some good players. Now that we've lost one, we're going to find out what we're made of. We have to get going and start another winning streak."

"The Giants might beat the Reds," Jenny said.

"Sure. That could happen. But we can't depend on it. We have to practice hard, and we have to beat them ourselves. We have to—"

"Coach, don't we get anything to drink today?" Billy Bacon asked.

Billy's timing was not good. A couple of the other players moaned.

"Hey, I only bring soda pop to winners," the coach said. Then he smiled and looked around. "And you guys are winners. Head for my van."

Everyone jumped up, and Jacob could tell they were feeling better already. But then he heard the coach say, "Kenny, I want to talk to you for a minute."

Kenny stayed behind, and Jacob waited not far away. The coach talked to Kenny for a few minutes, and then Kenny walked away, but not toward the van. He was leaving the park, heading home.

Jacob ran after him.

"What did he say?" Jacob asked.

"Nothing much."

"Come on, Kenny. Did he say you were in a slump?"

"No, Jacob, he didn't." Kenny sounded sort of mad. "He said I was trying too hard. He said I have too much pressure on me for a guy my age."

"Yeah, I know, but you've had pressure all year. But now your luck has gone bad. What you need to do is—"

"He says I have good mechanics—batting *and* pitching—but that I'm not as strong as those sixth-grade guys. He said not to worry about getting a hit every time—or striking guys out."

"That's true, Kenny. That's exactly right. But you hit that last ball a *mile*. You were just unlucky. Another foot or two and it would have been out of the park."

"Yeah, well, I should have taken a nice stroke and gotten a single—and kept the rally going. I tried to swing too hard."

"But it's luck, too, Kenny. Last week you would have hit the thing over the fence and been the hero. But now that you're in a slump, you just can't—"

"Jacob, I don't want to hear one more word about this stupid slump."

"But you've got to do more things to change your pattern. You never did try a rally hat."

"Oh, brother. Jacob, I'm never wearing my hat upside down. No matter what you say. And one other thing: no more pennies in my shoes. That stupid thing gave me a blister today."

"What about rubbing the catcher's head? You didn't even try that."

"You're off your rocker, Jacob. I'm going to practice hard and play better. That's all." And away he went, heading home without Jacob and Harlan.

"At least he's changing that pattern," Jacob whispered to himself. But then he hurried over to Harlan, who was at the van having a soda with everyone else.

"Harlan," Jacob said, "we can't give up. We've got to think of a way to help Kenny."

"Come on, Jacob, he'll be okay."

"What kind of an attitude is that? Just think how he stuck with us when we wanted to get our first hits. He threw pitches to us every night."

"Hey, I'll practice with him all he wants."

"He doesn't need practice. He needs to change his luck."

"Jacob, you're weird, you know it? How come you're so superstitious all of a sudden?"

"What are you talking about? This is changing luck—breaking slumps. If you're going to be a major leaguer someday, you have to know all this stuff."

"You mean grown-up guys do this stuff—wearing their hats wrong and all that?"

"More than just that. I heard about one player who drove a certain way to the stadium one morning and then went four-for-four. After that he drove the same way to the stadium every day for the rest of the year."

"And did he go four-for-four every day for the rest of the year?"

"No, stupid. It doesn't work like that."

"Well, then, what good does it do?"

"It brings luck. That's the whole point."

"If it brings so much luck, he ought to get four hits every day."

"Geez, Harlan, you don't get it. I doubt you'll ever make the majors with that attitude."

Harlan believed more in practicing than in luck. Jacob agreed that it couldn't hurt. And so on Thursday they took extra batting practice with the team, and on Friday they got some guys together and practiced even more.

Kenny was really ripping the ball. He seemed to have eased up on his swing, and he looked natural. Harlan was also looking better the more he practiced.

Jacob practiced hard too, but seemed to spend half the time changing things around.

He got guys to take their batting practice in a different order.

He talked some of them into running the wrong way around the bases a couple of times.

He even talked Eddie Boschi into walking backward to the plate when it was his turn to bat.

But he could tell that the other players just thought it was funny. No one was taking him seriously.

Mr. Sandoval stopped by on Friday night. He watched Kenny take a couple of swings, and then he said, "That's right, son. You look a lot better."

"Mr. Sandoval," Jacob said.

"Yeah."

"When you were in the majors, what did you do to break out of a slump?"

"Well, I wasn't around long enough to get in a slump," he said, and he laughed. "Maybe my whole career was a slump."

"But didn't some of the guys on the Dodgers do things to change their luck?"

"Oh, yeah. Just about all ballplayers do some of that stuff. I don't know if they really believe in it, but it's part of the game."

"What kind of stuff did they do?"

"Well, I knew one guy who used to go

over and touch the water cooler before he batted—just because he did that once and hit a grand slam."

"See, Kenny," Jacob said.

"And I knew another guy who ate a hot dog just before the game every night. He even had to buy it from the same guy. One night the guy wasn't there and he got all upset."

"I'll bet he had a bad night, too."

"I don't know. Seemed about the same as usual."

"Yeah, but it could have started a slump. That's how those things go."

Mr. Sandoval laughed. "I think maybe batting practice is more important," he said.

"Sure, but don't you think Kenny ought to try some new stuff—just to stop this bad string of breaks?"

"Yeah. I think he ought to swing easier and not throw quite so hard."

Harlan laughed, and so did Kenny.

Jacob didn't.

★ 6 ★

Jinx

On Saturday morning the Dodgers played the A's.

Jacob offered to come over to Kenny's house and help him think up more "changes." But Kenny told him to stay away. He would walk to the diamond any way he wanted—and wear whatever underwear he liked.

But Jacob had a few ideas. He had finally found a rabbit's foot. He thought he could at least talk Kenny into putting that in his pocket. And he thought maybe he could get Billy Bacon to rub his head against Kenny. But that might take some doing.

But when Kenny showed up for the game, Jacob could see that the problem might be bigger than he ever expected. Kenny looked nervous, even scared.

"What's wrong?" Jacob asked.

Kenny walked to the big canvas bag that the coach had just dropped on the grass. He pulled out the bats and other equipment, and found his favorite bat.

"Please use a different one today," Jacob said. "Will you?"

"*NO!*" Kenny said. "Leave me alone. I told you I don't believe in all that hocus-pocus stuff. I'm not changing *one thing*."

"Hey, why didn't I think of that? Good idea."

"What?"

"Try to go back to what you were doing before your slump. What did you do to get into it, anyway? Did you switch something that—"

"Jacob, get away from me."

Harlan had just walked up. "What's going on?" he said.

"Nothing's going on," Kenny said. "I'm just going to relax and have a good game."

"You don't sound very relaxed."

"That's because Jacob is driving me *crazy.*"

But Jacob knew what Harlan was talking about. Kenny hadn't been this uptight the night before.

"Kenny, what's going on?" Jacob asked.

"Nothing."

"Something is. Come on. You can tell us. We're your best buddies."

Kenny took a long look at Jacob and finally said, "I got this, but it doesn't bother me one bit." He pulled a slip of paper from his back pocket and handed it to Jacob.

The note was scribbled in pencil. It said:

In case you don't know how come you can't hit so good any more, its becus we put a jinx on you. It will last for the hole season. Nothing can ever ever stop it, no matter what. So get use to it. You thought you were a big hot shot, but you arn't, so dont ever think you are again.

"Where did you get this?"

"It was in my mailbox, in an envelope, with my name on it. But no stamp. Someone just put it in there."

"It's those stupid Giants," Jacob said. "It's the same kind of stuff Cranny was saying after the game."

"I know," Kenny said. "And there's no such thing as a jinx." He gripped his bat and pounded it on the ground. "So now I'm going to go get some batting practice."

Harlan said, "Kenny, the coach and your dad both said to relax. You're not relaxed now."

"*Yes, I am,*" Kenny said, and he slammed the bat on the ground again. "Those stupid Giants aren't going to make me think I can't hit. And Jacob, you aren't going to either."

"I didn't ever say that."

"Well, you keep telling me I'm in a slump. That's the same thing."

Kenny walked away, and for the first time Jacob realized that maybe he was part of

Kenny's problem. Maybe he was only making Kenny doubt himself.

And things got worse. A few minutes later
Kenny walked over and said, "The coach
doesn't think I can pitch anymore. He's
having Eddie start."

"That's because Bunson used up most of
his innings, and you don't have six left
either. He wants to see if Eddie can get by
for a while, and then he'll bring you in."

"Maybe. Or maybe he thinks I'll *walk*
everyone."

Wow! Kenny had never talked that way
before.

Jacob had to help him somehow, but he
had to think of a better plan. When he went
to the dugout, at the start of the game, he
didn't do much broadcasting. He had to
think.

Eddie started out the game by walking the
first A's batter. Jacob could tell how nervous the other Dodgers were as they paced
around at their positions in the field.

But then Eddie settled down and got the side out.

And that's the way the game went for a while. Eddie didn't look great, but the defense played well, and the A's didn't score.

But neither did the Dodgers. They loaded the bases in the second, and again in the third. But they couldn't get a clutch hit when they needed it.

Kenny was still trying too hard. He swung hard and barely topped the ball in the first inning. The ball rolled in front of the plate and the catcher threw him out.

In the third inning he came up with Henry and Jeff on base and did the same thing. Ground ball. Out.

Things were getting tense. The Dodgers just couldn't lose to the A's—they were probably the worst team in the league!

Jacob could tell that the other players were getting nervous. Poor Brian Waters had to take off for the men's room twice, and the first time he almost didn't make it back in time to bat.

But in the fourth inning Brian came through.

Eddie led off the inning with a fly ball for an out. But Billy socked a ground ball single and Brian came up with a chance to get something going.

Jacob could see that Brian was nervous. He could hardly hold still as he stepped up to bat. And then he bounced a little grounder to third.

But Brian was fast. Jacob watched him go all out as he sprinted for first base. The third baseman had to come in for the ball and then make a long throw.

"*SAFE!!!*" the umpire shouted.

"All right!" Jenny yelled. "Now we break out of our slump."

This was the first time anyone but Jacob had admitted that the team was in a slump. Jacob wondered whether he had planted the idea in their heads and made things worse.

Henry yelled back to the dugout, "Let's bat around this inning. Let's *all* hit."

But Henry never got a pitch he could drive. Suddenly, the pitcher couldn't get the ball over the plate, and he walked Henry. The bases were loaded.

As Henry ran down the first-base line, he looked over at the dugout. "Of course, we don't have to *hit* if he wants to *walk* us."

Everyone laughed and cheered. But Jacob thought he knew what they were thinking. They had loaded the bases before and hadn't scored.

And now it was Kenny's turn to bat.

Earlier in the season the other players would have been confident something good was about to happen. Now they sounded as if they were trying to convince themselves.

"Come on, Kenny," Sterling Malone yelled. "You can do it."

But Jacob had a plan. He just didn't know whether he dared use it.

It was the sort of thing that maybe he shouldn't . . .

But there was Kenny standing stiffly at the plate, looking as if he wanted to chop the ball in half.

The first pitch came in, way outside, but Kenny lunged and almost swung.

Jacob couldn't believe how tight he looked.

"Come on, Kenny, ease up," Bunson yelled. "Make him pitch to you."

Maybe it *was* time to try his plan. But Jacob would be taking a big chance. Kenny might react the wrong way and—

And then Kenny took a wild swing. He might as well have had his eyes closed. Kenny stepped back and slammed his bat on the ground. He looked mad enough to eat the thing.

All the A's were screaming, and Kenny was letting them get to him.

Jacob knew his plan was sort of crazy, but he had to do something.

"Time out!!!!" he yelled.

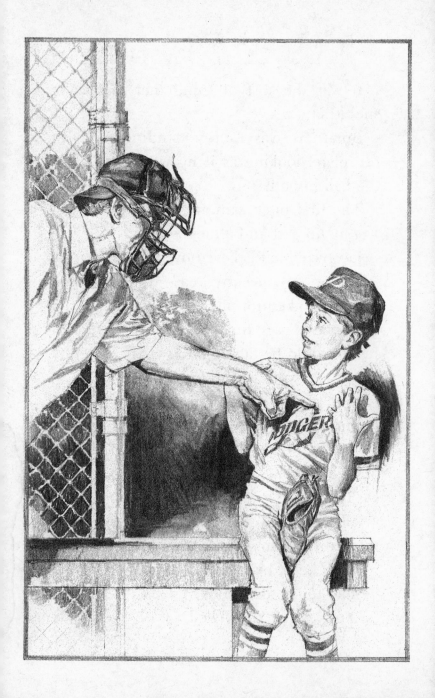

★ 7 ★

Super Play

Jacob ran from the dugout. "Coach," he yelled. "Take a look at that ball."

"What?" Coach Wilkens yelled back.

"Look at that ball they're using."

The coach walked toward home plate. The umpire was already looking at the ball. "There's nothing wrong with it," he said. Then he tossed the ball to Coach Wilkens.

The coach turned it over a couple of times, looking at it carefully. "What are you talking about, Jacob?" he said.

"Let me see it."

Jacob walked over to the two men. He

took the ball from the coach and looked it over, and then he turned around, as if he wanted to look at it in bright sunlight. When he turned around again, he said, "My mistake. It's okay."

That got a big laugh from the crowd, and a bigger reaction from the A's, who all started yelling at Jacob, telling him what a doofus he was.

But Jacob didn't care. He quickly walked over to Kenny, who had been waiting, looking disgusted.

"Kenny, I just pulled a switch. I changed balls. The new ball looks and feels normal, but it has a special core—like a Superball. All you have to do is meet it—just connect—and it will shoot clear out of here."

Jacob started to walk away, but Kenny ran after him.

"Come on, son," the umpire barked. "Let's get going."

But Kenny was whispering to Jacob. "You can't do that. It's cheating."

"I already did it."

"If we get caught, they'll kick us both out of the league."

"They won't catch us. You'll hit it so far they'll never find it. But just don't swing hard, or they'll see it doesn't fly like a regular ball."

"No, Jacob. I won't do it."

"Boys, that's enough. Let's get going here," the umpire said. He was walking toward them now.

"Kenny, you can't tell on me. They'll kick me out of baseball forever."

"I won't do it, Jacob. I'm not going to cheat that way. Tell the ump you want the ball back."

But the umpire was almost on top of them. "Boys, break it up right now or I'm going to call the batter out."

"I can't ask for it," Jacob said. "They'll know I did something. Go ahead and hit, but swing *really* soft. Then I'll think of a way to get it back out of the game."

"Jacob, that's still—"

"All right," the umpire said. "That's it. I'm—"

"No, sir. I'm coming." Kenny walked quickly to the batter's box. But he was watching Jacob.

He let the first pitch go by for a called strike.

Jacob wondered whether Kenny would swing at all. He made a motion to him—a nice, soft swing.

Kenny shook his head as if to say, "I don't like this."

Then he let another pitch go by. But this one was a little high.

Jacob made the motion again, and Kenny finally nodded.

The next pitch was fat, right down the pike, and Kenny took a nice, smooth swing.

The ball *shot* off his bat.

It screamed down the first-base line into the right-field corner.

Kenny probably could have stretched it

into a triple, but he was so surprised he ended up stopping at second.

All three runners scored.

Jacob was jumping up and down, celebrating with the rest of the team. But Kenny looked upset.

Jacob would tell him what had really happened as soon as he got a chance, and then everything would be okay.

But . . . Kenny was yelling something. The crowd was making so much noise Jacob couldn't—

Oh, no!

"Ump, time out," Kenny was yelling. "I have to tell you something."

Jacob was out of the dugout and running hard. He got to Kenny before Kenny passed the mound.

"Wait, wait," he said. He grabbed Kenny. "What's going on?"

"Boys, I've had about enough of this." The umpire was walking toward them.

So was Coach Wilkens.

Eddie Boschi was looking at Jacob as if he were nuts, and the whole crowd had gone quiet.

"Jacob, I can't do it. I'm telling them what we did. I'm not going to win a game that way." He looked up at the umpire, who was just a few feet away now. "Sir, we cheated. We used—"

"No, Kenny. No."

Jacob slapped a hand over Kenny's mouth. But Kenny pulled free.

"Sir, that ball wasn't—"

"Kenny, no. It was the regular ball. Really. I just told you that."

"What?"

Kenny turned and stared at Jacob.

"You've been swinging too hard. So I told you that it was a Superball so you'd swing easy. *And it worked!*"

Jacob could see that Kenny was trying to decide whether he believed him or not.

"I'm telling the truth, Kenny."

"Look, boys, if you pulled some trick with that ball," the umpire said, "you're in a lot of trouble." He was holding his mask in his hand and pointing a stubby finger at Jacob. He had the face of a bulldog.

Jacob was *verrrry* glad he hadn't really broken any rules. The umpire looked as if he could eat Jacob for lunch and still put away a nice dessert.

"No, I didn't. I just said I did. That can't be against the rules."

Now it was Coach Wilkens' turn to say something. "Jacob, you better explain—and quick." Then he walked the boys away from the umpire.

"I told Kenny I switched balls," Jacob said. "He didn't want to hit it, because it would be cheating. I knew he'd say that. So I said, 'Just hit it easy,' and he did. My plan worked."

"But that ball shot off my bat," Kenny said. "I don't think it was a regular ball."

"Sure it was. There's no such thing as a Superball that looks like a baseball. I just made that up."

"Why did it go so far then?"

"Because you connected. Because you didn't overswing. Because you finally did what the coach and your dad and everyone else has been telling you to do."

The ump was leaning in now.

"It was nothing," Coach Wilkens said. "Take a look at the ball. It's the same one you inspected just a minute ago."

Then, in a gruff voice, Coach Wilkens told Jacob, "I don't like that kind of stuff. You let me do the coaching, okay?"

"Okay," Jacob said.

Then the coach said, "Kenny, I'm proud of you. You were going to turn yourself in. You weren't going to cheat."

Kenny nodded, but he looked embarrassed. "It was a pretty good trick," he said. "It worked."

Coach Wilkens tried not to smile, but couldn't help himself. All the same, he told Jacob, "Get back to the dugout. Let's play some *baseball*."

Jacob ran back to the dugout, smiling all the way. When he got back the other players wanted to know what the heck was going on. But Jacob just kept smiling, and when he looked out at second base, Kenny was smiling too.

★ 8 ★

Back on Track

"Come on, Jacob, what did you do out there?" Henry wanted to know.

"Yeah. I heard you saying something about the ball," Billy said.

"Well, I'll just tell you this much," Jacob said. "Kenny is out of his slump. I think we all are. Let's get some *runs* now."

"*Yeah!!!!*" all the players yelled.

And another cheer went up when Malone drove the next pitch over the third baseman's head, scoring Kenny from second.

When he came running back to the dugout, everyone tried to get some answers out of him.

"I just got my swing back, that's all. Jacob told me something that helped me."

"What did he tell you?" Jeff asked.

Jacob was on deck, but he looked back at the players in the dugout and grinned.

"He just told me not to swing so hard. That's all there was to it."

"Everyone's been telling you that."

"I know. But Jacob made me believe it."

No one really understood that—except Jacob and Kenny—but it was okay. Jenny had just crunched one that whizzed past the shortstop before he could move.

And then Jacob came up and hit the longest shot of his life, a high drive over the left fielder's head that bounced up against the fence.

Jacob ran hard and stretched it into a triple.

Two more runs scored.

The Dodgers were on track again.

"The slump is over!" Jacob yelled from third

base, and that became their battle cry the rest of the game.

The Dodgers went on to win 10 to 0. Kenny came up again and stroked a perfect shot up the middle for a single. And then, when Eddie got himself in trouble in the fifth, Kenny came on to pitch, retiring the final five batters in order.

He didn't try to do more than he could. He just threw with his natural motion, and suddenly his control was back.

Harlan also got up in the fifth, and although he didn't get a hit, he was careful what he swung at, walked, and then came around to score. So he was feeling pretty good, too.

When Coach Wilkens talked to the players after the game, he told them he was glad to see them catch fire again.

"We needed a little something to get us going," he said, "and I guess sometimes it takes a trick or two." He laughed, and everyone wanted to know all over again what had happened, but the coach wasn't telling.

Jacob's dad came down after the game, beaming and shaking everyone's hand. He wanted to give the boys a ride home, but Jacob said they had better walk. "That's our routine after we win, Dad. We better not break it up. We're trying to get a new streak going."

"Well, all right," Mr. Scott said. "But I was thinking about ice cream cones."

Harlan and Kenny both looked interested, but Jacob said, "Another time, Dad. I really think we better not take a chance right now."

And so the rookies walked home together.

On the way, they finally told Harlan what had happened.

"Wow, Jacob, how did you ever think of that?" Harlan said.

"I don't know. I just knew that Kenny

wasn't going to listen to me if I talked about changing his luck, so I had to trick him into taking a different kind of swing."

"See," Kenny said, "it was the swing that made the difference. Not lucky pennies in the shoe or anything like that."

"What are you talking about?" Jacob said. "You've got a lucky rabbit's foot in your pocket right now."

Kenny reached into his pocket and found the furry foot on a chain.

"How did that get in there?"

"I slipped it in before the game."

"Well, it didn't do any good."

"What are you talking about?" Jacob said. "Your luck changed, didn't it?"

"Not for a while."

"Well, these things *take* a while sometimes."

The boys laughed, but Kenny finally said, "You don't really believe in all that stuff, do you, Jacob? There's no such thing as a jinx."

Suddenly Jacob remembered the note from the Giants. "Well, I don't believe someone can put a jinx on someone else. I just think rubbing the catcher's head or stuff like that—well, you know, it can't hurt. It's baseball tradition."

"I know what we ought to do," Harlan said. "We ought to write a letter to the Giants and say, 'Our slump is over, and we don't believe in jinxes. So look out.' Something like that."

Jacob started to laugh. "I got a better idea," he said. And then he stopped, right on the street, in the middle of town. "We ought to send a letter, say it's official from the league, and say, 'If your catcher, Mr. Cranny Crandall, does not take a shower before the next game, the Giants will be *disqualified* from the league.' "

Harlan liked that one. Kenny did too.

They walked on, laughing, and Jacob knew things were definitely looking up.

"Hey, I got another hit today," he said finally. He had sort of forgotten about it in the excitement over Kenny's slump ending. "A *triple!*"

"I know," Harlan said. "And I didn't drop a single ball at first base. We're all getting better. I think we're going to be *stars* after all." He leaned his head back and laughed in that cackling voice of his.

"Yeah, that's right. But that's not what I mean," Jacob said.

"What are you talking about?" Kenny asked.

"I'm on a streak. I've had hits three games in a row now."

"Yeah, that's good."

"Not just good. I gotta think about everything I've been doing. I have to wear the same socks, and I've got to come to the park the same way again next time, and . . ."

Kenny and Harlan cracked up, but Jacob kept right on talking, mostly to himself.

"Let's see, what did I have for breakfast? Oh, and I know what else. In every game I've got to call time out, and maybe I ought to tell Mom not to wash my uniform."

"No—that's going too far," Kenny said.

But they all laughed. It was nice to be talking *streak* again—instead of *slump*.

BOX SCORE, GAME 8

Paseo A's 0   Angel Park Dodgers 10

	ab	r	h	rbi		ab	r	h	rbi
Boston ss	2	0	1	0	White 3b	3	2	2	2
De Klein cf	2	0	0	0	Reinhold 2b	3	1	1	1
Bessant 3b	2	0	0	0	Sandoval ss	4	1	2	3
Smith c	2	0	0	0	Malone cf	3	1	2	1
Sullivan lf	3	0	1	0	Roper 1b	4	1	3	1
Oshima 2b	1	0	0	0	Sandia lf	2	0	0	0
Santos 1b	0	0	0	0	Boschi p	3	0	0	0
Watrous p	3	0	0	0	Bacon c	2	2	2	0
Chavez rf	1	0	0	0	Waters rf	1	1	0	0
Trout rf	2	0	0	0	Scott lf	2	0	1	2
McConnell 2b	1	0	0	0	Sloan rf	0	1	0	0
Powell 1b	1	0	0	0	Bunson lf	1	0	0	0
ttl	**20**	**0**	**2**	**0**		**28**	**10**	**13**	**10**

A's   0 0 0 0 0 0—0
Dodgers 0 0 0 6 4 x—10

League standings after eight games

Dodgers	7–1
Reds	7–1
Giants	5–3
Padres	3–5
Mariners	2–6
A's	1–7

Sixth game scores

Dodgers	11	Padres	5
Giants	6	Mariners	4
Reds	12	A's	4

Seventh game scores

Giants	7	Dodgers	5
Reds	11	Mariners	7
A's	5	Padres	2

Eighth game scores

Dodgers	10	A's	0
Padres	6	Mariners	3
Reds	7	Giants	5

DEAN HUGHES has written many books for children including the popular *Nutty* stories and *Jelly's Circus*. He has also published such works of literary fiction for young adults as the highly acclaimed *Family Pose*. When he's not attending Little League games, Mr. Hughes devotes his full time to writing. He lives in Utah with his wife and family.

ANGEL PARK ALL-STARS #1

Making the Team
by Dean Hughes
**They aced the tryouts—but
can they win over their teammates?**

Kenny, Jacob, and Harlan are the youngest Little
Leaguers to make the Angel Park Dodgers. They're
all anxious to prove themselves to the older guys,
but they haven't counted on the antagonism of
team slugger (and bully!) Rodney Bunson. He'll do
anything to stay on top. Can the rookies survive
Rodney's version of hardball? Can the Dodgers?

BULLSEYE BOOKS PUBLISHED BY RANDOM HOUSE, INC.

ANGEL PARK ALL-STARS #2

Big Base Hit
by Dean Hughes
He really needs one—or he may be off the team!

His buddies Kenny and Jacob, the other third graders on the team, have already gotten their hits. Harlan knows he won't really feel like an Angel Park Dodger until he gets his. But no dice. The harder he tries, the worse it gets. Soon everyone's starting to worry—especially Harlan. What if he *never* gets a hit? What if he doesn't belong on the team after all?

BULLSEYE BOOKS PUBLISHED BY RANDOM HOUSE, INC.